SIX STOREY HOUSE

SIX STOREY HOUSE

Written by
Geraldine McCaughrean

Illustrated by
Ross Collins

Hodder Children's Books

a division of Hodder Headline Limited

First published in Great Britain in 2002
by Hodder Children's Books

10 9 8 7 6 5 4 3 2 1

A Catalogue record for this book is available from the British Library

ISBN 0 340 85407 3

Printed and bound in Great Britain
by Clays Ltd., St. Ives plc

Hodder Children's Books
A division of Hodder Headline Limited
338 Euston Road, London NW1 3BH

For Rachel, Helen and Juliette

Contents

Chapter One
Dexi
page 9

Chapter Two
Box and Cox
page 17

Chapter Three
Widow Shoo
page 31

Chapter Four
Mr Tring's Lament
page 47

Chapter Five
The Four Quarters of Mr Somerville
page 59

Chapter Five-and-a-bit
Behind Closed Doors
page 73

Chapter Six
Spots
page 77

Chapter Seven
Dexi's Plan
page 89

Chapter Eight
A Model Tenant
page 99

Chapter Nine
All Change
page 107

The Extension
page 121

Chapter One
Dexi

Six Storey House stands in its little garden like a potted palm: tall and thin and brownly dusty. Once, a single family lived there. They kept servants in the loft, where other people keep luggage, and a cook in the cellar, where other people keep wine. Now each floor has a different address: Flats 1 to 6, Six Storey House.

Dexi lives on the third floor, with his mother. Each day, when he comes home from school, he lets himself quietly in at the big brown front door (for fear of waking Cox) and climbs the stairs to Flat Three.

"Hello, I'm home!" he calls,

but he knows there will be no answer. His mother goes out to work. She leaves his tea in the microwave, like a canary in a cage.

But Dexi doesn't mind. Sometimes, after tea, he goes to see Mr Somerville who lives on the ground floor – or Mr Tring on the fourth. And sometimes he goes to see Mrs Shoo who lives on the second. Sometimes he passes Box or Cox on the stairs, coming or going. The only person he never visits is Mrs Groner at the top of the house, because Mrs Groner never opens her door. Occasionally Dexi sees her black cat slip slinkily by, but never Mrs Groner.

With so many neighbours, Dexi is rarely lonely. Of course, if he had a horse, he would never be lonely at all, but perhaps a third floor flat is not the ideal place for a horse. Whenever he mentions a horse to his mother, she only shakes her head and sighs.

Every night, Dexi's mother comes home from work and sighs. She is too tired to look for words, too tired to talk or play or read stories – too tired to do anything but eat and sigh and go to bed.

Chapter Two

Box and Cox

Box and Cox share the first floor of Six Storey House. But they only own one bed. They only need one bed. Cox works nights and Box works during the day. When Box is working, Cox is sleeping. When Cox is working, Box is sleeping. They pass each other on the tall front steps, Cox stretching, Box yawning. They pass each other twelve hours later, when Cox is pooped and Box is still wiping the sleep out of his eyes.

And, though they are friends, they hardly ever speak. Instead, they leave notes on the fridge door:

No butter.

Your turn to pay the milk.

There is something green in the larder.

Sadly, they work so hard that they never have time to mend the dripping tap, or patch the peeling wallpaper. They never have time to nail down the squeaky floorboards or glaze the broken window. It isn't that they can't afford the repairs. Cox is a builder and Box can turn his hand to anything. It is just that between working and sleeping, they never have the time.

Once, last year, Box was given the job of demolishing a burned-out shop in Grime Street: Number Nine. Rolling out of bed, washing his face at the dripping tap, he set off for work. All day he worked, with crowbar and sledgehammer, reducing the ugly, blackened building to a pile of bricks and timber. By evening, he could not wait to get back to Six Storey House and bed.

Cox, meanwhile, rolled out of bed, combed his hair in the cracked mirror and set off for work. He, too, had work in Grime Street, building a shop at Number Six. Sure enough, there, in the lamplight, beyond the gate marked No 6, he found a rubble-filled space, and all night long he worked, laying bricks, laying floors, raising roof beams and rafters. By morning, he could not wait to get back to Six Storey House and bed.

In he came, too weary to eat, saw the soft dip in the creased pillow, lay down on a sheet still warm, and slept.

That night, he went back to Grime Street. He found the place where Number Six should be. But instead of walls and floors and roofbeams, all that he found was a heap of rubble.

All night he worked to put right the damage, mixing mortar, planing wood, sinking drains, and by morning he was almost too tired to eat his fish and chips.

But the very next night, the house was gone again: a heap of rubble, a gap like a missing tooth in the jaws of Grime Street.

"This is terrible! This is a

disaster! I'm finished!" he cried. All night long he worked with a heavy heart. In the morning he even stopped Box on the tall front steps of Six Storey House and told him: "Tragedy! Disaster! I've lost all of my skill! I've forgotten my craft! Everything I build falls down again! Who is going to employ a builder who can't build?"

Box said, "Very sorry. Can't stop. Big job on. Shoulda finished yesterday. Sleep well."

All day Cox tossed and turned in the crumpled bed. He dreamed of dinosaurs eating his house, of rain dissolving houses like sugar lumps. He dreamed of giant pigeons perching his house flat. He dreamed earthquakes.

When he woke up, Box was shaking him. "My turn. Get up. Terrible day. Worn out. This job. On and on."

Plop went the dripping tap. Bang went the broken window. The house was weary, too.

All week, Cox went to work and found Number Six in ruins.

All week Box went to work and found he still had work to do on Number Nine. Harder and harder they worked, until both felt sure they had lost all their skill.

"I give up," said Cox and sat down on the steps. "I thought I knew how to build a house, but I'm nothing but a miserable failure."

"Give up," said Box and sat down beside him. "Always thought. Demolition work. Easy."

So they agreed to swop.

Cox would go to Number Nine, Grime Street and knock it down during the day. Box would go to Number Six and build it during the night.

It was odd for Cox to be out during the day. He felt like a mole above ground. It was odd for Box to be out at night.

He missed the traffic and the passers-by and the warm sun on his vest.

One week later, on a Saturday morning, Dexi found Box and Cox sitting on the steps of Six Storey House crying bitterly and sharing one dirty handkerchief.

"What's the matter?" asked Dexi.

"Failure," said Box

"So am I, too," said Cox.

"Skill gone," sobbed Box.

"So has mine, too," sobbed Cox.

They explained to Dexi about Number Six which kept falling

down, and Number Nine which refused to be demolished. "We're finished," said Cox. "We may as well retire and go to live in Spain."

"Let's go and see," said Dexi.

Dexi walked round to Grime Street. "If I had a horse," he said, "we could have ridden here."

"It would need to be a big horse," said Box and Cox, yawning and taking it in turns to blow their noses.

They found the place where a heap of bricks lay like a box of broken biscuits.

"This is it," said Box and Cox, both together.

"Number Six," said Cox.

"Look at the gate post."

"Number Nine," said Box "Between Seven and Eleven."

Dexi put one finger in the loop of the metal number on the gatepost and turned it the right way up.

"You knocked down my house!" said Cox.

"Undid all my work!" said Box. "Ought to punch you on the nose."

But they were both laughing too much to do anything of the sort.

There was no more talk of retiring to Spain. In fact there was not much talk at all. Number Six Grime Street was built and Number Nine Grime Street was knocked down. Cox went back to working by night and Box by day, and neither had a moment to mend the dripping tap. They were both far too busy earning money by the hodful.

Chapter Three

Widow Shoo

Widow Shoo, on floor number two, has no money at all.

She has eleven growing children, twelve beds, twenty-one shoes, twelve nappies, a pushchair and a pram in the hallway, but no money.

She has huge meals to prepare, but the cost of fish-fingers frightens her more than tarantulas, and her cupboards are often bare. She has heaps of mess to tidy away, but no food to put on the table. Every day she does a tubful of washing, but has too little space to dry it.

Sometimes Dexi helps out after school, filling the washing

machine, sorting clothes into whites and coloureds, matching socks, searching for the baby in among the ironing. But there is nowhere – absolutely nowhere – to hang all the washing.

"If I had a horse," says Dexi, "I would ride your washing over to the launderette," he says.

"I can't afford the launderette," says Widow Shoo.

Once, Widow Shoo hung the socks on a tree in the street . . . but the birds came and nested in them before they were even dry.

Once, she took a ride on the bus and each of the children let the washing flap out of the window. But Mrs Shoo had forgotten they would all need to pay the bus fare. So they got turned off the bus at the gasworks, and had to carry the washing all the way home.

Once, she hung the washing on the telephone wires outside Six Storey House, but for some reason Mr Tring threw open the window and shouted that she would break his heart if she did not take it down again.

So Widow Shoo's flat is always draped with washing. Dexi likes it like that. "It looks like a row of Arabian tents," he says.

"Arabian tents aren't cold and clammy," says Widow Shoo. "It's bad for the baby's cough."

But, in some ways, the baby's cough is useful. He is a good baby and does not cry. If it were not for his cough, Dexi might never find him in among the washing.

Each morning, Widow Shoo sends two children off to big school, two to junior school, two to the infants and two to nursery. It still leaves a handful, but Widow Shoo can find room for them. She is a very tidy person. (She needs to be.) Min goes in the bouncer, Sonny goes in the playpen, and the baby goes in the pram. Then Widow Shoo is ready to start work.

To earn money, Widow Shoo does little jobs for the other tenants of Six Storey House. She picks up Mr Tring's untidy papers, cleans his bath, polishes his tuba and triangle, oils his drumskins and whitens the piano keys with lemon juice. She times his metronome and tunes his tuning fork; she irons his flats and sharpens his sharps.

Meanwhile, Min bounces, Sonny plays and the baby sleeps, as good as gold, in the pram, coo-ca-choo, blowing bubbles.

Next, Widow Shoo tidies for Mr Somerville. She makes his bed, moves his chair, cooks his breakfast and puts his paints in order: Red, Orange, Yellow, Green, Blue, Indigo, Violet.

"Stay and model for me," says Mr Somerville. "I'll paint your portrait and call it Supershoo!" But Widow Shoo is far too busy. She has to hurry upstairs and check that Min is bouncing, Sonny is playing and the baby is happy, coo-ca-choo, blowing bubbles.

Next she cleans for Box and Cox (though she has to put on carpet slippers and creep about, for fear of waking Cox). She picks up their picks, tidies their trowels, sets their saws' seventy teeth, irons their oily overalls and polishes the dripping tap. She has even been known to change the bed while Cox is sleeping in it!

Widow Shoo cleans for Dexi's mum, too. She does not clean for Mrs Groner, of course, because Mrs Groner won't open the door, but she sometimes feeds the Cat Groner when it is out and about. Widow Shoo is very fond of cats.

Then it's back upstairs to praise Min's bouncing and Sonny's playing and to feed the baby in the pram, coo-ca-choo.

*

"Time for your feed," said Widow Shoo to the baby one day. And the baby opened a pair of green eyes, waved a long tail and, jumping down from the pram, ran away upstairs.

"Oh soap-and-water, I've lost the baby!"

Widow Shoo tried to remember whether she had tickled a baby or a cat, whether she had burped a baby or a cat, whether she had dandled a baby or a cat, whether she had *seen* a baby or a cat asleep in the pram. But in her fright she could not remember. So back she went to

Box and Cox and searched
among the saws and under the
overalls to see if she had hidden
the baby away among the

hardware. There was no baby to be found.

She searched among the rainbow paints and in all four quarters of Mr Somerville's flat, but the baby was nowhere to be seen.

She searched Dexi's flat in case she had tidied the baby away with the Lego, the comics or the cereal dishes. But no baby.

"I'll help you look," said Dexi, who had come home from school for his lunch.

Together they searched Mr Tring's room – under the tuba, inside the piano – while Dexi made helpful suggestions.

"Perhaps you oiled the baby and changed the drumskin. Maybe you polished the baby and burped the tuba? You might have tuned the baby and . . ."

But there was no baby in Mr Tring's flat, though they searched as high as Top C and as low as a double bass.

They even went and called through Mrs Groner's door. *"Have you seen my baby, Mrs Groner?"*

Mrs Groner growled back, "No babies in here, thank goodness! Go away! . . . Oh, and who's been putting talcum powder on my cat, I'd like to know!"

Widow Shoo sat down on the stairs and wept into her apron. "I've lost the baby! Oh! What a wicked woman I am!"

"Think back," said Dexi. "Before you cleaned the flats, what did you do?"

"I took the children to school, put Min in the bouncer and Sonny in the playpen."

"Nothing else?"

"Well, I hung up the washing, of course."

Down the stairs ran Dexi and rummaged in the laundry basket. He startled Cat Groner secretly snoozing among the laundry, smelling of talcum powder. But there was no baby in the basket. Dexi looked in the peg bag, but though he found safety pins instead of pegs, there was no baby.

He looked out at the trees, where the sheets billowed like ghosts. He looked out at the bushes, where the socks hung like early Christmas decorations. Then he looked at the line – that little length of washline looping over the brown lawn. And there, between the nighties and the napkins, between the bloomers and blouses, between the tablecloths and towels, pegged up by its nappy, hung the baby, fast asleep.

*

"*Oh baby, baby, baby!* What kind of mother have you got?!" cried Widow Shoo when Dexi brought back the baby. "Come here and be tickled and dandled and fed, and tell me you love me, my own little love!"

"*Burp!*" said the baby.

Then Dexi supposed that, although it was hard for the Widow to have so many children, it must be much better than having one too few.

Chapter Four

Mr Tring's Lament

Mr Tring has no problem with his washing. It is his music which drapes and droops around the fourth-floor flat of Six Storey House.

Mr Tring plays sad, soulful music at the Opera House, though lately his conductor has not been too happy with his playing. How could anyone be happy hearing Mr Tring play? He plays such sad and soulful music on his triangle.

Dexi wonders if Mr Tring really enjoys playing the triangle.

"No. I used to play the piccolo," says Mr Tring, "but it made dogs gather on the front steps and howl. For a while I played the violin, but it made Widow Shoo's baby cry.

"I tried the drums, but Mrs Groner banged on the floor with her walking stick, and she would bang in 15½ beats to the bar." Telling Dexi this makes Mr Tring sadder than ever.

He has not always played sad music, just as he has not always played the triangle. "Once I planned to write great music," he tells Dexi, ". . . but now I never shall."

Sitting one day in his bath, Mr Tring looked out of the window and saw . . . music. He blinked twice, thinking he must have imagined it, but no. There was music written in the sky outside his bathroom window.

A flock of sparrows were perching on the telephone wires, some as big as crochets, some as little as grace notes. They huddled in trilling cadences, between the top wire and the bottom, just like notes on a stave. And when Mr Tring hummed their music, it was the most beautiful melody he had ever heard.

Slowly, slowly, he slithered out of the bath. A sudden

movement might startle the birds. In any case, they might flutter off their wiry perch at any moment. He had to be quick and stealthy.

So, teasing the toilet paper off its holder, he wrote down the tune, note by note, using a piece of green soap for a crayon. *"Pom pom-petty pom ti pa-pah."*

The red roof of a double-decker bus; the roar of a motor bike . . . Up flew the sparrows, like rice at a wedding, and wheeled away across the sky, leaving the phone wire blank. Mr Tring did not care.

"Pom pom-petty pom ti pa-pah," he hummed, flourishing the

soap. The toilet roll was empty. The bathroom floor was full. But Mr Tring had composed his masterpiece!

By this time his teeth were chattering and his skin was turning goosey with cold. Jumping and skipping and singing for joy, he ran to find a towel. He must copy out his masterpiece! He must run to the music shop, buy some paper, copy out the tune and turn it into a symphony! The Sparrow Symphony! Ode to Sparrows! Birdhaven's Fifth!

Wrapped in a towel, Mr Tring ran all the way to the music shop

and all the way back, paper riffling like sparrow feathers. He ran up the tall front steps and all eight flights of stairs.

The door to his apartment stood open. Mrs Shoo had been in to clean.

His cereal bowl was washed up. His bed was made. There was

no dirty ring round the bath. There was no toilet paper on the bathroom floor.

"NO!" It could not be true. *"Bomti papa poppety,"* sang Mr Tring under his breath, but his heart was beating to the wrong rhythm and his memory was rattled about by running.

"Bom pippety poo-pah . . . NO!!"

His symphony was gone – as surely as the dust from his coffee table and the sparrows from the wire.

He waited at the window every day for a week, hoping the sparrows would settle again. On the Sunday they mustered in the sky. One by one they began circling downwards. *Pom pom-petty . . .*

Then Widow Shoo, down on the floor below, opened her window and, with a long pole, began trying to fling her washing over the telephone wires.

Mr Tring gave a loud scream. "You have broken my heart!" he cried.

Then Mrs Groner began knocking on the ceiling, 15½ beats to the bar. Somewhere in the house, a tap was dripping in waltz time. Mr Tring's misery was complete.

After that, he never played anything but sad, soulful music, blipping his triangle like a prisoner clanging on the bars of his prison cell.

Chapter Five

The Four Quarters of Mr Somerville

Mr Somerville lives on the ground floor of Six Storey House. He cannot manage the stairs any more. Every lunchtime and every evening, the pizza shop on the corner sends round a pizza. Dexi thinks Mr Somerville must like pizza very much indeed, to eat it twice a day. Quite often, he gives Dexi a slice left over from lunch.

There are four rooms on the ground floor. In the morning, he sits in the room facing east. "I call it the Morning Room," he tells Dexi.

In the afternoon, he sits in the room facing south. "I call it the Sun Lounge," he tells Dexi.

In the evening he sits in the kitchen, because it faces west. "I call it Sunset Boulevard," he tells Dexi.

Mr Somerville's bedroom faces north. At least Dexi supposes it must face north, because Mr Somerville calls it the North Pole. But there is no window, so it's hard to be sure. Sometimes Dexi wheels Mr Somerville's chair from the Sun Lounge to Sunset Boulevard and they sit there together in the fading light, Mr Somerville drawing horses for Dexi in the margins of the evening paper.

"Why do you move around

from room to room, Mr Somerville?" asks Dexi.

"I follow the sun," says Mr Somerville.

"But the view's just the same!"

This is true (except for the north side where there is no view at all). A high garden wall surrounds Six Storey House, so whichever window Mr Somerville looks out of, he sees the same pattern of grimy red bricks.

"Ah, but the light, Dexi! The light!" says Mr Somerville. "The sunlight changes fifty times between dawn and dusk. In the morning it tastes of lemonade and by the evening it's strawberry."

Dexi sits with Mr Somerville and the gloom settles round them, but Mr Somerville never puts on the lamp until it is too dark for them to see each other.

A few years ago, Mr Somerville was a professional painter. He painted landscapes and portraits, cartoons and posters. And, because he was a painter, he put his name in *Yellow Pages* under 'Painters'.

A lady rang with a voice the colour of plums, and said, "I want you to paint my house."

So that's what Mr Somerville

did. He set up his easel on the pavement outside her house, and he painted it, in oils, on canvas. It was a fine, bright picture, perfect in every detail, from the mauve plastic milk-holder to the orange chimney pot. He even included the lady herself, in her crab-pink curlers, shouting at the postman. He painted the birds all flying away as she came stomping down the drive.

"Who are you and who said you could paint my house?" demanded the woman with the plum purple voice.

Mr Somerville was perplexed, but he reminded her of the

telephone call and showed her the picture (which was very good).

"What a stupid man you are!" said the woman in a voice the colour of raspberries. "I wanted my house painted, not a painting of my house!"

Mr Somerville (whose mother had taught him very good manners), blushed deeply.
"I am so very sorry, madam. I quite misunderstood. I shall begin work at once."

He went home and borrowed a ladder from Cox and Box. He had just set it up against the wall of the lady's house when she sallied angrily out of the front door (almost knocking Mr Somerville off his ladder).
"I'm going shopping, man," she declared. "I trust you will have it finished by the time I get back!"

So Mr Somerville worked fast, and he made such a fine job

of the house that passers-by stopped to admire his work. The neighbours came out to stare. Cars driving by tooted their horns to see such lovely painting.

Mr Somerville painted a big tree against the wall of the house and filled it with green parrots and blue monkeys. He painted a big bright sun on the roof tiles and a big black crow on the chimney pot. He painted a cobra clinging to the drainpipe and a waterfall cascading most realistically out of the gutter. The people who had gathered in the street began to murmur and shout suggestions.

Mr Somerville painted the windows a transparent blue and filled them with fishes. He perched a pelican on the porch, and gambolling lambs on the garage.

When the lady came back from shopping, she could not see the house at first, such a crowd had gathered on the pavement outside. Some had been home for cameras and stepladders to stand on. Children sat astride their fathers' shoulders.

The lady stuck out her elbows and pushed past. Jabbing at people with a small umbrella, she carved her way through the crowds to her front gate.

Strangely, when she saw what Mr Somerville had achieved, she was no more pleased then before. Her face changed to an interesting mandarin colour. "*What have you done to my house*?" she wanted to know – which was silly because it did not take much intelligence to see that Mr Somerville had *painted* it.

By now, the crowd had started to cheer and to clap. They were delighted with the eagles painted on the eaves, the sunset painted on the west wall. They picked up Mr Somerville and carried him shoulder-high all round the garden, while the lady jumped about waving her umbrella.

"I can only think that the poor lady forgot she had asked me to paint her home," Mr Somerville told Dexi. "I know she had a poor memory. After all, she couldn't even remember my name."

"Why? What did she call you?" asked Dexi.

"All *sorts* of things," said Mr Somerville and there was a certain shy twinkle in his grey-green eyes.

Chapter Five-and-a-bit

Behind Closed Doors

Mrs Groner hates the sunlight, whatever flavour it happens to be. Daylight hurts her eyes.

Mrs Groner hates music, because it frays her nerves.

She loathes Widow Shoo's children when they slam doors. She hates Six Storey House, because sometimes, when the traffic roars by outside, the walls shake and the windows rattle in their frames. Even the noise of a tap dripping somewhere in the big old house has her chewing the corners out of her lace handkerchief.

To tell the truth, Mrs Groner hates a lot of things. But, most of all, she hates to be interrupted, so she never answers the door. Even her door has no letter box. The only time she unfastens the latch is to let her cat in and out.

So Dexi does not know any stories about Mrs Groner. He has lived all his life in Six Storey House, and still knows nothing at all about Mrs Groner on the fifth floor.

"I'm sure she must like horses, though," he thinks to himself. "*Everyone* likes horses."

Chapter Six

Spots

One day, Dexi came home from school with spots. He had spots behind his knees, in his ears, under his shirt. There was a noise in his head like a dripping tap.

He sat on the tall front steps and thought what to do with his spots. He did not go to help Widow Shoo drape her washing or sort her socks. He did not go and sit with Mr Somerville or listen to Mr Tring playing the triangle. Instead, he went indoors and sat on the stairs and, when Box came home from work, gave some of his spots to him, though Box did not notice at the time. When Cox came out, ready for work, Dexi gave him spots as well (though he seemed to have just as many himself afterwards).

It was not that he wanted Box or Cox to feel bad. It was just that he had a plan, and the plan called for spots.

"I have a plan," Dexi told his mother when she came home.

"Plans can wait," said his mother. "It's bed for you."

When Box and Cox got measles, they could not go to work either by day *or* by night. Box came home and found Cox in bed and shook him. "Wake up. Want my bed. I'm ill."

"I'm ill too. Can't you see the spots?" said Cox.

So Box had to climb in to the other end of the bed and, heel to heel, they stared at the unpainted ceiling. The ceiling too seemed to have spots.

The tap dripped, the door banged, the window rattled and the paint continued to peel.

"You know what?" said Cox. "That tap needs a new washer."

"Door needs a new catch," said Box.

"The ceiling could do with a coat of paint."

"Stairs squeak, too. Ever noticed? Stairs squeaking?"

"I'll fix them when I feel better."

Meanwhile, the phone began to ring in the hall. Widow Shoo went to answer it. It was a man wanting to know why Box had not laid his crazy-paving path.

"Mr Box is ill just now," said

Widow Shoo. "A crazy-paving path, is it? Now, I could do you one of those this afternoon. With eleven children, I'm a dab hand at piecing together broken bits."

She left the children with Mr Tring (because Dexi had spots) who taught them music,

to pass the time.

He taught the baby to clap, the crawler to croon, the bawling one to bang, the little ones to la la and the bigger ones to boogie. He taught them the solfa and the salsa, to hum and to rumba. He taught them to blow trumpets and suck flutes, to strum guitars and pluck sitars.

It drowned out the sound of Box nailing down the squeaky floorboards. It drowned out the dripping tap. But nothing could muffle the din of Mrs Groner banging on the floor, 15½ beats to the bar, out of time with the music.

The children fell silent, staring up at the trembling lampshade.

Dexi, tucked up in his measly bed, scratched between the spots and fell asleep wondering where the drips from that tap all ran down to.

The next time the phone rang, it was a woman wanting to know why Cox had not come to mend her washing machine.

"I know more about washing machines than Mr Cox will ever know, poor soul!" said Widow Shoo. "Tell me where you live and I'll come right round."

She left the children with Dexi (because Dexi's spots had almost gone) and, when his mother came home, she found a baby in the laundry basket, a crawler under the couch, a crier in the cupboard and a giggler playing the pans. There were a couple of schoolboys doing homework and a schoolgirl learning her lines. There was a minx climbing the curtains and an angel licking up crumbs.

"Crumbs?" called Dexi's mum above the din.

"I made them a picnic," said Dexi.

Dexi's mum gathered all the

children together and read them a story. While she read, the only sound was the distant dripping of a tap and the tap-tapping of Cox and Box as they mended their broken window.

Chapter Seven

Dexi's Plan

It was the silence which woke Dexi. Nowhere in the whole house was there a dripping tap, a banging door, a rattling window, a clonking pipe. Box and Cox had put everything to rights.

What is more, they had been down to the cellar to check the wiring and damp-proof the walls, and up on to the roof to fix the TV aerial.

"This place could be better," said Cox to Box.

"Much," said Box.

"It could be very comfortable, in fact," said Cox to Box.

"A palace," said Box.

So they worked on, painting

the staircase, mending the front steps, unblocking the gutters.

"Did you find out where all those drips ran down to?" Dexi asked as he steadied their ladder.

"Into the cellar," said Box. "All mopped up now, though."

"Could someone keep a horse down there?" asked Dexi (who never gave up on a dream).

"No, no," said Cox. "A horse needs sunlight. No windows in the cellar. No sound, no sunlight, nothing . . . I said to Box, I said, 'It's like the bottom of a mine down here.' Didn't I say that, Box?"

"You did, Cox. You said, 'Like this bottom of mine'."

"Not *my* bottom, you fool! A *mine's* bottom!"

Dexi left them arguing, and crept down the cellar steps. As he clinked on the light, a NEW plan glowed in his head like a light bulb.

When Dexi had his Great Idea, he told Mr Somerville and Widow Shoo. He told his mother and Mr Tring. But how could he tell Mrs Groner?

There was no letterbox on her door.

The windows were too high to reach.

He called through the

keyhole and he knocked on the knocker. But Mrs Groner only shouted back, "Go away! Leave me alone! Stop your noise and rattling!"

Dexi waited on the landing, but Mrs Groner was too quick for him. She opened the door a crack, and Cat Groner slid slyly out and went shimmying down the stairs.

All day Dexi waited and then all night, torch in hand, until the green glitter of feline eyes came sprangling up the stairs. Then, quick as a flash, Dexi pounced! He poked his note under the cat's collar.

To Mrs Groner: please read.

Cat Groner's claws scratched on the door of the topmost floor. Quick as a mouth, the door opened and shut. In went the cat and in went Dexi's note. There was the sound of bolts shooting and chains being fastened.

"Will she read it?" called Mr Tring feebly from the landing below.

"Fingers crossed!" called Widow Shoo, putting on her bicycle clips, ready to go to work.

"Won't she just tear it up?" said Cox to Box.

"Or not even see it?" said Box.

"Will she think it's a joke?" said Dexi's mother, cuddling four spotty Shoo children and rocking the pram with her foot.

"Will she open the door, at least?" said Dexi, yawning. It had been a long night.

The chain rattled on Mrs

Groner's door. The bolts banged back. The key clicked. The latch lifted. Wide as a rat's armpit, the door opened, and a shaft of electric light fell across the landing. There stood Mrs Groner in her dressing gown and dark glasses. Crumpled in her hand was Dexi's note.

"The answer's no," she said. Then, pointing at Dexi with a long pale finger, she beckoned him inside.

Chapter Eight

A Model Tenant

Dexi found himself standing in one large room lit by only one light bulb. All the curtains were drawn and the skylight was blinkered with blinds.

There, in the middle of the room, stood a huge model of the Taj Mahal, made entirely of shining, silver, wound, linked, twisted and intertwined paper clips. He gave a gasp of admiration, hardly daring to breathe. "It's beautiful!"

"It's not finished yet," said Mrs Groner. "Every time a truck goes by, or those Shoo children slam the door, or that music vibrates, or a draught gets in, domes fall down and walls crumble. The work of years is undone."

"I see," said Dexi, in a whisper.

"Twenty years I've been building it. And you want me to MOVE?"

"The place I'm thinking of is stony quiet," said Dexi. "It's pitchy black with the light off. There are no draughts and no vibrations."

Behind her dark glasses, Mrs Groner closed her eyes. She looked like a woman imagining a tropical island.

"Ah, but the *stairs*, boy,"

she groaned. "The *stairs*! We would never get my model down the stairs!"

"Aha!" said Dexi and gave a cunning smile. "But there's a LIFT now. Box and Cox just finished installing it."

Carefully, carefully, they picked up the Taj Mahal. Gingerly, gingerly, they carried it out of the flat. Box and Cox had to take the doors off their hinges before it would fit through.

It slid into the lift with never a hair's breadth to spare. Cautiously, cautiously, they slid shut the lift doors. Fingers

crossed, eyes closed, they pressed the button.

Down slid the lift, with a click and a whirr, into the newly painted cellar – and, after the Taj Mahal came Mrs Groner's bed and table, desk and dresser and carpet. Into the cellar went 150 jumbo boxes of paper clips, reels of thread, boxes of Cornflakes. Box and Cox carried, while Mr Tring conducted, and Dexi's mother made sandwiches, and Mrs Shoo's children admired the model of the Taj Mahal from beyond the cellar door. Even Mr Somerville rolled his chair out into the hall to gaze down the cellar steps.

"Hello, Mr Somerville," said Dexi. "You're next."

Chapter Nine

All Change

The day Dexi lost the last of his spots, his mother burst into tears.

"I'm sorry. Should I try to catch something else?" asked Dexi, baffled. "Did you like me better with spots?"

"I like you with and without spots," sobbed his mother. "But now you are better I'll have to go back to work, and then I hardly ever *see* you."

"Why not stay home, then, and look after Widow Shoo's children?"

Dexi's mum shook her head. "I have to earn a living," she sighed.

"Oh, Widow Shoo has plenty

of money to pay you," said Dexi.

"She *does*?"

It was true. Widow Shoo was so good at doing Box and Cox's jobs that people were begging her to build their garages, knock down their shed, clear their lofts, soundproof their cellars. She proved particularly good at designing schools and playgrounds. Dexi's mum said that probably had something to do with having eleven children.

Box and Cox didn't mind her doing their work. They were still busy, planting out a roof garden on top of Six Storey House. Soon the roof billowed with washing, and Mr Tring was up there, head lost among the flapping nappies, practising the drums, the bagpipes and the tuba.

With Mrs Groner and the Taj Mahal safely installed in the cellar, Mr Somerville was able to move into the topmost flat. After all, the lift could take him right to the door.

No curtains, no blinds, no garden wall. In all directions, he could see as far as the edge of town. Even in the middle of the room, he found that the travelling sun spilled its flavours into his lap: lemonade from the east, orange juice at noon, strawberries from the west, milk from the north. And at night, as he lay in bed, his skylight was full of stars.

Mr Somerville was a happy

man. "If I were a cat (he said to Dexi) I would purr like that one out there." And he pointed through the window at a cat in the topmost branches of a tree.

Just then, there was a knock at the door. It was Mrs Groner.

Dexi's heart missed a beat. "Perhaps she wants her flat back!"

But no.

"I've lost my cat!" said Mrs Groner. "I've looked everywhere!"

Nobody had thought to tell Cat Groner about the swapping of flats. Climbing the stairs, finding a stranger in its home, it searched Six Storey House for Mrs Groner

– searched the lobby, searched the stairs, looked in the laundry baskets and in Widow Shoo's pram. It looked on the sills and out in the garden and finally, in despair, it climbed the tall tree whose branches spread out alongside the topmost window. From there, it might at least squinny in at the window and find out what had happened to Mrs Groner.

It found no Mrs Groner . . . but it did find out that it could not get down.

They spread out one of Widow Shoo's sheets, like a cradle, to catch Cat Groner. "Now, when I give the signal," said Dexi, "try to make it jump!"

The children banged the dustbins, Mr Somerville flashed sunlight off a mirror, Mrs Groner tinged the feeding bowl, while Mr Tring made loud burping sounds on a tuba. Nothing happened.

Box and Cox brought a ladder.

Up went Dexi.

"Do be careful, Dexi!"

– past the porch roof,

– past the double-glazing of Box and Cox's apartment,

– past the bird-feeder stuck

to Widow Shoo's window,

– past the horse posters stuck in his own window,

– past the wind-harp hanging in Mr Tring's open window,

– past even the curtainless windows of the topmost flat, where Mr Somerville sat watching anxiously from his chair.

"Do be careful, Dexi boy," said Mr Somerville.

The birds in the tree took one look at Dexi and flew up in a fountain of feathers. But Cat Groner sat on Dexi's shoulder all the way down, claws digging in deep, her whiskers tickling his ear.

Dexi was half expecting a cheer. He was hoping for a round of applause. But as he reached the ground, there was not a murmur, not a sound. He turned around and found the residents of Six Storey House with their fingers to their lips, their faces turned up to the sky. Only Mr Tring was busy, writing on the wall, with a paintbrush from Box's box.

He was painting music.

Dexi looked up at the telephone wire and there, sure enough, were the birds he had scared out of the tree. Some as fat as minims, some as small as grace notes, they perched on the wires like notes on a stave of music, and the tune that they made was being immortalised by Mr Tring, across the front of Six Storey House.

It trilled through the honeysuckle, it roared round the roses:

"Pom pom-petty pom ti pa-pah!"

It even crescendo'd across the nameplate of the house.

"Can't read the name now," said Box to Cox.

"That's all right," said Dexi, "It had to be changed anyway." And the others agreed with him.

It was Seven Storey House now . . . at the very least.

The Extension

Box and Cox are still extending the house – a cinema, skating rink, conservatory; the swimming pool and bistro; the pavement art gallery and the bandstand. Dexi's mother runs the bistro. She does a good trade, what with the crowds who come flocking to see Mrs Groner's version of the Taj Mahal, now that it is finished.

Box and Cox say their improvements to Seven Storey House are only the beginning.

But Dexi is already content. The stable on the roof is just what he needs, since his noble horse shows no fear of heights and always behaves well in the lift.

There is a room free on
the ground floor now, of course.
Do you think you might be
interested?

May I show you around?
FLAT FOR SALE
SEVEN STOREY HOUSE

The End

Geraldine McCaughrean

writes books for readers of
all ages. She has won many prizes,
including the Whitbread Children's
Award (twice), the Library
Association Carnegie Medal, the
Guardian Award and the Blue Peter
Book of the Year Award.
She has also retold hundreds of
myths, legends, folktales
and literary classics.